The Berenstain Bears
and the
TROUBLE WITH FRIENDS

When making friends,
the cub who's wise
is the cub who learns
to compromise.

A FIRST TIME BOOK®

The Berenstain Bears
and the
TROUBLE WITH

Stan & Jan Berenstain

FRIENDS

Random House 🏠 New York

Copyright © 1986 by Berenstain Enterprises, Inc. All rights reserved. Published in the United States by Random House Children's Books, a division of Random House, Inc., New York. Random House and the colophon are registered trademarks of Random House, Inc. First Time Books and the colophon are registered trademarks of Berenstain Enterprises, Inc. randomhouse.com/kids
BerenstainBears.com
Library of Congress Cataloging-in-Publication Data
Berenstain, Stan. The Berenstain bears and the trouble with friends. (A First time book)
Summary: Lonely without friends her age to play with, Sister Bear is delighted when a new little girl cub moves into the house down the road.
ISBN 978-0-394-87339-8 (trade) — ISBN 978-0-375-98251-4 (ebook)
[1. Play—Fiction. 2. Friendship—Fiction. 3. Bears—Fiction.]
I. Berenstain, Jan. II. Title. III. Series: Berenstain, Stan. First time books.
PZ7.B4483Beks 1986 [E] 85-30165
Printed in the United States of America 72 71 70 69 68 67 66 65 64 63 62 61

Sister and Brother Bear, who lived with their mama and papa in the big tree house down a sunny dirt road deep in Bear Country, were not only sister and brother, they were playmates and they got along pretty well—most of the time.

But Brother was quite a lot older than Sister—almost two years—and sometimes he wasn't much interested in the games she wanted to play. Especially when Sister got a little bossy—which she sometimes did.

"Now," she said one day as she came out of the tree house with a big armload of her dolls and stuffed animals, "we're going to play tea party. You sit there and be the papa and I'll sit here and be the mama."

"Aw, gee, Sis," said Brother. "I'm too old to play tea party. Why, if Cousin Freddy or any of the guys saw me I'd never hear the end of it. Why don't you find somebody your own age to play tea party with?"

"Besides, I have a date to go skateboarding with Freddy." And off he zoomed, leaving Sister all by her lonesome.

"All right for you!" she shouted.

"Oh, dear," said Mama, who was watching from the tree house window. "There goes Brother off to play with Freddy again. I do wish Sister had somebody her own age to play with."

"What about her school friends?" asked Papa, joining her at the window.

"They all live too far away," sighed Mama as she watched lonesome Sister pick up her trusty jump rope and start jumping with a friendly frog. Soon a butterfly joined in.

"She has her forest friends, the frogs and butterflies, to play with," said Papa.

"Frogs and butterflies are all very well," said Mama. "But they're not the same as having a cub friend your own age."

That's when Mama saw the moving truck out of the corner of her eye.

"Look!" she said. "A new family moving into the empty tree house down the road! It certainly would be nice if they had a cub Sister's age."

Sister saw the truck too—and the car following it.

"Somebody moving into the empty tree house!" she said. "I wonder if they have any cubs." And off she skipped down the road to investigate.

The truck stopped at the empty house and the moving bears began to unload it. The car pulled in behind the truck and the new family got out. There was a mama, a papa, and a little girl cub just about Sister's age!

Sister could hardly believe her good luck! Just what she needed—a little girl cub to jump rope, play tea party and house and school, and have all kinds of cub fun with! She could hardly wait to say hello. She skipped over and introduced herself.

"Hi! I'm Sister Bear. I'm six years old and I live just down the road."

"Hi!" said the new cub. "I'm Lizzy Bruin and this is my papa and mama, Mr. and Mrs. Bruin. I'm six years old too. May I try your jump rope? I can do Red Hot Pepper!"

And could she ever! Lizzy Bruin was the fastest rope jumper Sister had ever seen.

"I can jump to a thousand," said Sister.

"I can do a thousand and one," said Lizzy, returning the rope.

"A thousand and two," snapped Sister.

"A thousand and three," said Lizzy.

"Well, we'll just see about that! Let's have a jump-off here and now!" said Sister.

"Let's not and say we did!" said Lizzy. "Say! Isn't that a playground over there? Last one there is a rotten egg!" And off she ran with Sis doing her best to catch up.

"Well," said Mama, who had been watching from the window, "the new cub certainly is a lively little thing. She may be just what Sister needs."

Sister and Lizzy had quite an afternoon. They climbed to the top of the junglegym…

rode the seesaw…

and pushed each other on the swings.

They played tag...

laughed and giggled...

rolled down a grassy bank...

and picked wild flowers for their mamas.

"Why, thank you, Sister. How lovely!" said Mama, putting her wild flowers in water. "Well, what's your new friend like?"

"Her name is Lizzy, she's six years old, she's an only cub—and," Sister said, "she's a little bossy."

"Oh," said Mama. "Well, you certainly seemed to be having fun."

"Oh, yes!" said Sister. "I had a lot of fun! A little bossy—*and* a little braggy."

The next morning, bright and early, the phone rang. It was Sister's new friend, Lizzy.

"Want to come over and play school?" asked Lizzy.

"Okay," said Sister.

"Bring some of your dolls and stuffed animals," added Lizzy, "because mine aren't unpacked yet."

So Sister gathered up some of her favorite dolls and stuffed animals and headed for the tree house down the road.

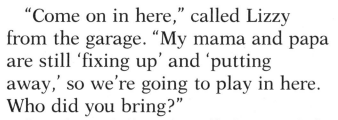

"Come on in here," called Lizzy from the garage. "My mama and papa are still 'fixing up' and 'putting away,' so we're going to play in here. Who did you bring?"

"My best doll and stuffed animals," said Sister. "And this is my special teddy that I've slept with every night since I was a baby."

Lizzy had set up the garage like a schoolroom. There were boxes for the pupils to sit on, and there was another box for the teacher's desk. There was even a blackboard and chalk for lessons.

"This is going to be fun," thought Sister Bear as she began sitting her toys on the boxes. That's when she heard the tapping sound. It was Lizzy tapping on the desk. She had a pretend pointer in one hand and a piece of chalk in the other.

"Please be seated, Sister. It's time for your lessons. Today I'm going to teach you the alphabet. The first letter of the alphabet is—"

"Now, just a minute!" protested Sister. "Who said you were going to be teacher? When I play school *I'm* the teacher! And not only that—I already know my ABC's!"

"Sister Bear, if you don't sit down this minute, I'm going to keep you after school!" said Lizzy.

"Is that so?" shouted Sister. "Well, if you don't give me that pointer, I'm going to keep *you* after school!"

That's when Sister grabbed the pointer. Soon they were rolling around on the floor wrestling for the pointer, which broke in two.

"Now look what you did!" shouted Lizzy. "You broke my best pointer!"

"I'm not going to play with you ever again!" shouted Sister, gathering up her toys. "I'm going to take my dolls and go home!"

"Sister's mad and I'm glad!" shouted Lizzy as Sister marched out of the garage.

"Lizzy Lizzy in a tizzy!" Sister shouted back.

"Back so soon?" asked Mama when Sister returned looking like a storm cloud.

"I'm never going to play with that Lizzy Bruin again!" shouted Sister. "She's much too braggy and bossy! I don't need her to play school or anything else! It's much better playing by yourself! When you play by yourself you can do what you want when you want without having to worry about that Lizzy Bruin!"

"That's true," said Mama in a quiet voice. "Of course, there are some things you really can't do very well by yourself."

"Like what?" asked Sister.

"You'd have a pretty hard time pushing yourself on a swing," said Mama. "And I'd like to see you ride a seesaw by yourself. Most games like hopscotch and jacks take at least two to play. And it certainly is nice to have someone to laugh and giggle with."

"Maybe so," said Sister, "but Lizzy is much too braggy and bossy. Why does she have to be the teacher when we play school?"

"It seems to me," said Mama, taking Sister on her lap, "that Lizzy isn't the only cub that's braggy and bossy sometimes— and, of course, there is one thing you can do much better by yourself."

"What's that, Mama?"

"Be lonesome," said Mama quietly.

And that's when somebody knocked on the door.

It was Lizzy and she was carrying Sister's teddy.

"When Sister took all her dolls and went home, she forgot her teddy," she said. "And, well, I knew it was her special favorite that she slept with since she was a baby and I thought she might miss it."

"Why, thank you, Lizzy," said Mama. "That was very thoughtful of you."

"Thank you very much," said Sister, hugging her teddy.

"And you can be teacher if you want to," said Lizzy.

"Or," said Sister, "we can take turns being teacher."

"Terrific!" said Lizzy.

"Great!" said Sister, gathering up her doll and stuffed animals again. "Last one back to your garage is a rotten egg!"

And off she scooted,
laughing and giggling,
with Lizzy scampering
after her.